One Witch

Laura Leuck

Illustrations by S. D. Schindler

WALKER & COMPANY ◆ NEW YORK

For Will. —L. L.

First published in the United States of America in 2003 by Walker Publishing Company, Inc.

Published simultaneously in Canada by Fitzhenry and Whiteside, Markham, Ontario L3R 4T8

For information about permission to reproduce selections from this book, write to Permissions,
Walker & Company, 435 Hudson Street, New York, New York 10014

Library of Congress Cataloging-in-Publication Data

Leuck, Laura.
One witch / Laura Leuck ; illustrations by S. D. Schindler.
p. cm.
Summary: A witch goes around to her fiendish friends—from two cats to ten werewolves—
to gather the ingredients to make gruesome stew for her party.
ISBN 0-8027-8860-2 — ISBN 0-8027-8861-0 (rein)
[1. Witches—Fiction. 2. Halloween—Fiction. 3. Counting. 4. Stories in rhyme.] I. Schindler, S. D., ill. II. Title.

PZ8.3.L54943 On 2003
[E]—dc21
2002191049

The artist used ink and watercolor on watercolor paper to create the illustrations for this book.

Book design by Victoria Allen

Visit Walker & Company's Web site at www.walkerbooks.com

Printed in Hong Kong

4 6 8 10 9 7 5 3

One witch
on a hill
had an empty pot
to fill.

Two cats
inside a pail
gave the witch
a fish's tail.

Three scarecrows
stuffed with straw
gave the witch
a blackbird's claw.

Four goblins
eating bugs
gave the witch
some slimy slugs.

Five vampires
on the loose
gave the witch
some fresh blood juice.

Six mummies
wrapped in cloth
gave the witch
a musty moth.

Seven owls
wide awake
gave the witch
a rattlesnake.

Nine skeletons
on a stone
gave the witch
a finger bone.

Ten werewolves in a group

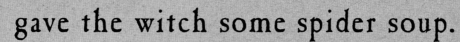

gave the witch some spider soup.

That witch
with her stash
began to plan
her spooky bash.

She took her bag,
dumped her haul,
then sent her trusty bats
to call . . .

ten werewolves
in their caves,

nine skeletons
in their graves,

eight ghosts
where they rest,

seven owls
in their nest,

six mummies
in their tombs.

five vampires
in their rooms,

four goblins
in their holes,

three scarecrows
on their poles,

two cats
near their can,

as one witch

then began

to mix and stir
her oozing stew.

She boiled and burned
her gurgling goo.

What did all
her good friends do?

They came and ate
that gruesome brew.

(Everybody
loved it too!)
They saved the last bowl
just for . . .

YOU!